FAMILY FARM

TO THE MICHAEL JOHNSON FAMILY

None of my friends sit with their sisters on the school bus, and neither do I. But the day we heard that our school was going to be closed, I did.

"Sarah, you said they'd never close down our school!"

"Leave me alone, Mike," she said, and she stared out the window.

"Why couldn't they close the school in Warren instead, and make those kids ride to our school? I don't want to sit on a bus for three hours every day! How are we supposed to have enough time to do our chores?"

"How should I know, Mike?" Sarah answered. "I guess we'll just have to get up earlier."

As soon as we got home, Sarah went looking for Mom. She was out in the garden, gathering the best pumpkins for tomorrow's trip to the market. Sarah told her the terrible news.

Dad and Grandpa had driven to town to deliver the last load of our corn crop, so I just started in on my own chores.

Before supper Sarah and I went out to the barn to work with our calf, Derinda. We groomed her and tried to lead her around on the halter rope. Then we tried to get her to drink milk from the pail.

"Come on, Derinda," Sarah said, "you're too old to be drinking from that big baby bottle."

"She'll never win a ribbon at the fair if she doesn't start growing soon," I said.

Then we heard the brakes on our grain truck squeal as Dad and Grandpa pulled up.

"Suppertime!" Mom called.

Dad and Grandpa were really quiet at supper. When I told them about our school closing, Grandpa just said, "With so many folks giving up and moving away, we'll be lucky if there are enough children left to fill the Warren school."

"You can't blame the farmers," Dad said. "The money we got from our corn crop today hardly covered the cost of seed, and gas for the tractor. And the price you get for milk these days is still way too low." He glared at Grandpa, then added, "If we had bought that land last year, maybe we could have raised enough to stay in farming."

"If we had bought that overpriced land, we would be bankrupt by now!" Grandpa snapped.

"Now, Pop, please don't start that again!" Mom said. "Things have got to get better." She turned to Dad. "Honey, do you think you could find a job to see us through until it's time for spring planting?" she asked.

"Maybe," Dad said.

That night I was so worried, I couldn't sleep. I saw a light on in Sarah's room, so I tiptoed past Mom and Dad's room and tapped quietly on Sarah's door. "Come in, Mike," she whispered.

"Sarah, if we lose the farm, what will happen to the animals? Where would we go? Would we have to move to the city?"

Sarah shook her head slowly and said, "We can't! What about Grandpa? He's lived his whole life on this farm."

Mom must have heard us. Opening the door, she said, "It's late, and you both should be asleep. Remember, tomorrow is Saturday, and we're taking a load of pumpkins to town. And don't worry," she added gently. "Somehow we'll find a way to keep the farm going. We always have."

A few years ago, when the bills started to pile up, we had to borrow from the bank to keep the farm going. Mom had wanted to get a job at the restaurant in town, to help out, but Dad didn't want her to do that. So last spring Mom planted a big garden of flowers, and pumpkins to sell at Halloween.

After morning milking we loaded the cool, slippery pumpkins in the pickup truck and drove to town. Nearly everyone wanted our pumpkins! "I can't believe it!" I told Mom and Sarah. "We sold every one!"

"And the florist asked us to bring more flowers," Sarah added.

When we got home, Dad said, "Pumpkins sure sell better than corn!"

"Then why don't we plant pumpkins?" Sarah asked.

Dad shrugged. "Selling a few pumpkins is one thing, but how would we sell thousands of them?"

A few weeks later my uncle Charlie, who is a foreman at the electric switch factory, helped Dad get a job. Our family was lucky because there weren't many jobs around.

On Dad's first day on the job I set my alarm to ring at five o'clock, an hour earlier than usual. Sarah and I would have to help Mom and Grandpa do the morning chores that Dad usually did.

Sarah is a sleepyhead. She hates to get up in the morning.

"Wake up, Sarah," I called.

"Go away! It's still dark!"

But finally she got up, and we went out into the pasture and brought in the cows. Grandpa turned the radio on to the gospel music station, as he always did, and he and Dad started milking.

When they were finished, I got a pail of milk for the barn cats. Just before he left for work, Dad called to us: "Thanks, kids! See you tonight."

It was tough keeping the farm running with Dad away all day. Grandpa cleaned the barn after milking, and he hardly ever went into town to drink coffee at the café with the other retired farmers. He worked all day. Sarah quit the volleyball team so we could both come home right after school. I decided not to try out for the basketball team this year. We took care of the calves and fed the pigs. The days were growing shorter and the sun was down when Dad got back for the evening milking.

Winter came. The old furnace at school wasn't working well, and some days it was really cold in our classroom. So the school boards decided that instead of getting a new furnace, we should start going to the Warren school right after Christmas vacation.

Changing schools didn't turn out to be so bad. It was fun meeting all the new kids from Warren. The gym was much newer, and everyone said that we would have a great basketball team. And the bus ride wasn't really that much longer.

One evening before supper Sarah and I were out in the barn feeding the calves. Derinda was finally growing, but we hadn't had much time to work with her.

"If we don't start getting Derinda to lead on the halter, she won't have a chance to win a ribbon at the fair," I told Sarah.

"I know," Sarah said, "but there just isn't enough time. It'll be great when spring comes and Dad can work full-time on the farm again."

But in February things started to get even worse. First Grandpa hurt his back and couldn't work. Our neighbors helped, but it was Mom who kept things going.

Corn prices were still low. Dad said it wouldn't pay to plant a crop, and he'd have to keep on working at the factory.

But things were slow at the factory, and we heard rumors that they might start laying off workers. If that happened, Dad said we'd have to sell the farm and move to the city, where he could find work.

Mom cried a lot and said, "We can't just give up!"

Then Sarah got a great idea. We decided to wait for just the right time to tell Dad.

The spring thaw began, and one warm Sunday morning we decided to walk to church. On the way back Sarah asked, "Dad, if we can't earn enough from corn this year, why don't we plant flowers and pumpkins? Mike and I could set up a farm stand by the main road and sell them to all the people that drive by."

Grandpa said, "You know, I've been thinking about pumpkins. A few fields might just make the difference for a farm like ours. But we might have to sell some of them to the food stores."

"We didn't have any trouble selling everything from the garden last fall," Mom said.

"We'd have to sell an awful lot of pumpkins to make a go of it. Do you really think we could do it?"

"I think so," said Grandpa.

"I'm a dairy farmer," said Dad. "I don't know anything about flowers or pumpkins."

"We can learn," Mom said.

We talked and talked. Then, when Dad got laid off at the factory, that did it! We decided to give it a try. We planted enough hay, oats, and corn to feed our animals through the winter, and the rest we planted in pumpkins and flowers.

By June the first seeding of flowers were in bloom, but so were the weeds. I couldn't believe how much work it took to raise flowers. We had to weed by hand, and spray and feed those plants all the time.

"If we were trying to grow weeds instead of flowers," Sarah said, "we'd be rich!"

When summer vacation came, we had a lot more time. But Sarah was never around—she and Grandpa were always driving somewhere to deliver truckloads of flowers—so I had to try to train Derinda by myself.

That summer my legs had finally gotten long enough to reach the clutch pedal on the old tractor. Dad started to teach me how to drive.

As we drove past the flower patch I saw that some of the flowers were withering. "Dad, a lot of the flowers are spoiling in the field. I know we're selling some, but do we earn enough to pay for the gas it takes to haul them?"

"Don't worry, Mike," he told me. "We've made some money on the flowers and now we know a lot of store owners who will sell our pumpkins at Halloween time. You know, we might just do all right."

Summer ended, and except for thousands of bright orange pumpkins, the color faded from the fields. Dad and Grandpa went back to all the stores that had bought our flowers and delivered tons of pumpkins. Sarah and I set up the roadside stand, and by Thanksgiving most of the pumpkins were gone! Dad and Grandpa even started talking about renting some land to plant a crop of Christmas trees.

We took Derinda to the fair, but when it was our turn to lead her past the judges, she balked and kicked. It was lucky I had a good grip on the rope. She didn't win anything, and we brought her home and put her with the rest of the dairy herd.

We were disappointed, of course. But a few days later, as we were closing the pasture gate, Dad called to Sarah and me, "Come to the barn. I have something for you."

There, nestled in the straw, was a beautiful newborn calf, who could win a ribbon at next year's county fair!